Elinor Sweetman

Footsteps of the Gods

And other Poems

Elinor Sweetman

Footsteps of the Gods
And other Poems

ISBN/EAN: 9783337158118

Printed in Europe, USA, Canada, Australia, Japan

Cover: Foto ©Andreas Hilbeck / pixelio.de

More available books at **www.hansebooks.com**

FOOTSTEPS

OF THE

GODS

AND OTHER POEMS BY

ELINOR SWEETMAN.

LONDON: GEORGE BELL AND SONS,
YORK STREET, COVENT GARDEN.
MDCCCXCIII.

TO MY SISTER AGNES.

[MRS. EGERTON CASTLE.]

HOW oft in childish days of yore,
When we were summoned down in state,
I trembling on the stair would wait
And push you through the drawing-room door.

But you returning drew me on,
Till I too braved the strangers' gaze,
And shared the smiles your brighter ways
And steps more confident had won.

And now on unfamiliar floors
Their rights the old sweet habits claim,
And I would call upon your name
As once in days of pinafores.

That I through you may entrance win,
And standing where you stood before,
Without the great unopened door,
May hear the voices cry : " Come in ! "

CONTENTS.

CONTENTS.

FOOTSTEPS OF THE GODS

AND OTHER POEMS.

———

FOOTSTEPS OF THE GODS.

THIS is the young Spring's dawn !
Over our wintry nakedness is drawn
A brown and purple veil of cradled buds ;
In the long ripples of subsiding floods,
Where dripping osiers shiver in the blast,
A downy brood is hatched from willow-wands ;
And through the skeleton splendours of the past,
The fern uprears its carven crosier-fronds.

Over is the night,
Out of darkness breaketh light,
Out of silence many-woven song.
Once more upon the dewy hill-top falls
The tread of mighty footsteps, and the sound
Draws from its hidden fountains underground,
The pulsing crystal stony veins along.

B

Life in the speckled shell begins to beat
Mid sprouting leaves ; and roseate daisy-balls
Dimple the valleys where the young lambs bleat.

Lo ! they are here,—the immortal gods are here !
With the first freshness of the new-born year,
They have remembered them the days of old,
When freely through the morning world they
    strode,
And earth their garden was, and they abode
Beside the sun on mountain summits gold.
Lo ! they are here once more !
And Nature too remembers steps she loved,
And the deep fires, within her bosom, moved,
Break unrestrainèd forth, the meadows o'er.
Cool flames of living emerald that creep
From bank to bank along the river's edge,
Fanned by a breath divine, then sportive leap
To twisted lines of beauty in the hedge,
Thence gain the forest whose long glade upheaves
Kingcups like showered sparks on ivy leaves.

In happy dawns,
When space on space is stirred with sound of
    wings,
As wider air through freshening branches swings.

And long blue shadows tremulously sway
Like floating lattices on drenchèd lawns,
They pass, the blessed ones, at break of day.
Is this the world we know?—these shining fields ?
These gilded woods ?—this unsubstantial plain ?
What peace is here !   What height of lonely
    air !
What gulfs of darkness every bush beneath
Make endless night along the bramble wreath,
As if for hours some mighty form had lain
Couched in the spice each tender sapling yields !
This is the wood-god's lair.
Where on the cold sweet grass, reclined at
    ease,
He piped unseen to wandering Dryades.

Boughs in the orchard close
Flushed with a faint and fleeting loveliness !
Meet fane for Aphrodite !—here she rose,
When April drifting down the green recess
Upbroke in foam its lowly arches o'er.
Like music, like a dream, like morning's breath,
Through swathes of herbage newly laid in death,
She wandered early down its tufted floor,
Pausing to bend in jest a rosy ear
To silent flower-shells ;—see how the pear

Is flecked with bud, where Eros hovering
Brushed the slim branches with a fleecy wing !
Further afield are languid wind-flowers frail,
Veined like the lids of young Endymion's eyes,
And sheets of springing primroses that wear
The colours of the moon in tearful skies ;
Perchance on such as these Diana stept,
When first, apparelled all in glories pale,
She stooped to kiss her shepherd as he slept ;
So much celestial sweetness lingers there.
Ah, Dian ! fled for ever are those days
When thou didst quit the midmost heavens pure,
To watch beside the timid mountain fawn,
Half-hid in odorous myrtle-boughs, and lure
Through trembling gates of sleep thy lover's
          gaze !
Who now beholding thee remotely thread
In cold serenity the golden maze,
To silver secret bowers overhead ;
Or through torn midnight's cloudy lattice wild
Show a white face austere, and swift withdrawn,
Could dream that thou on mortal youth hadst
          smiled ?

Gone is the olden time,
Blind faith and large simplicity sublime,

When fancy sang and graver tones were mute.
Ours is the riper age ; the hard round fruit,
The bearded fields that sober seasons bring ;
But who will give us back the bloom, the bliss,
The stir, the flush, the ecstasy of Spring !
Only with April's kiss,
Olympus, shaken through its weight of snows,
Wakes yearly from impassive deep repose ;
And youth undying, splendour, vigour, grace,
Roll from its misty summit into space :
So full a tide of life that it would seem
Not sap but ichor runs beneath the sods !
Behold they come ! they people Nature's dream—
But now they come unseen,—the scornful gods !

O, Poet ! doth thy heart within thee leap,
To whose keen sense these quickening days
      unfold
Brief touches of a long-forgotten race?
Or wilt thou weep ?
Knowing the world can never more behold
Its strong immortal beauty face to face.

•

ALCESTIS.

READ me this riddle, love. That, though thou
    wert
Alpha and Omega on earth to me,
I yet should measure what I feel for thee,
More by th' unfathomed anguish of my heart,
Now we are parted, than by joys sprung forth
From moments in thy lovèd presence spent ;
For if a prize be ours we are content
As far as in us lies,—some more, some less,
Our souls scarce reach as high as happiness,
But if we lose it, life is nothing worth.

Last eve I had a dream within a dream,
Upon a sunny hillside as I lay
Mid rocks and fern, where, with declining day,
Shadows of trees beneath me stretched away,
Like wandering paths across the golden gleam.

And in my dream I knew I was alone,

And knew that sometime in the bitter past
God's messenger had come for thee, and I
With breaking heart had watched thee breathe
    thy last,
And, bowed upon thy pillow, seen thee die.

Methought I heard the insects' busy drone,
And felt the sunshine slide along my breast,
Unconsciously, and I had ceased to weep ;
And yet I slumbered not, for that the stone
They set above thee in thy place of rest
Weighed over heavy on my heart for sleep.

But dimly through the languor born of tears
I knew a careless nature's ebb and flow,
The stir, the warmth, the tramp of mountain-
    steers
To cries from valley-pastures far below,
And all the insolence of life around ;
The same we used to love—the same !—and thou
Wert lying in the darkness underground !

O not the same ! for heaven's blue lay hid
In those lost glances 'neath thy coffin lid !
And hateful seemed the green, familiar earth,
And swallows' chorus of insensate mirth ;

The voice of waters, down their rocky shelf
Low murmuring of long monotonous glee,
Fell tunelessly upon my stricken ears ;
Spake I of life?—The whole world died with thee,
And I, lorn, desolate, accurst, lived on,
Chained to a lampless length of barren years ;—
I, whose own soul seemed alien to itself,
Loathing all things on which God's daylight
          shone,
And seeing all distorted through my tears !

This is the bitterness of loss ;—to strain
Our aching senses through relentless void,
Yearning for knowledge, yearning, but in vain,
For answering signs that love is not destroyed.
From those mysterious lands comes no reply ;
Naught save our own blind piteous tones again,
Naught save the echo of our baffled cry.

My longing pierced the solemn sunset air :
" O love, O love, how hath it fared with thee?
So cherished, watched, and guarded here, who
          yet
Wert summoned forth alone !—Canst   thou
          forget ?
Canst thou be happy seeing my despair ?

Did winged seraphs on the heavenly stair
Waft into space each lingering last regret,
Ere making thee of starry cities free ?
Or if in holy twilight aught of stain
Upon thine angel innocence detain
Thee prisoner for a while, is this thy pain
To know my loneliness ?—or dost thou wear
For home and love and all we used to share
A spiritual robe of white disdain ?"

Lo ! as my soul in deepening anguish fell
From gloom to nether gloom of sorrow's hell,
Where faith lay sick with doubt and wild alarms,
And every fiend had leave my thought to rack,
For one brief moment thou wert given back,
Like lost Alcestis, to my empty arms.
Yet, as I clasped thee,—even as I felt
Beneath thy kiss my hideous burthen melt,
Yea, ere the blessed vision fainter grew,
I was not all deceived, for that I knew
Such bliss intense, such bliss without alloy,
So full, so pure, we may not call our own.—
I did but dream.   This agony of joy
Was never mine in happiest days by-gone !

SONNETS.

I.

FIRSTLINGS.

THE joy of babes that see the primrose dart
Its first sweet rays o'er banks where winter lies,
The joy of those who under alien skies
Behold strange lands from distant waters start,
And shores unknown drive sea and sky apart,
All joys were mine of all discoveries,
When through my fitful April shone thine eyes :
First friendship is the primrose of the heart.

O lady mine ! the birds have ceased to sing,
The crops are garnered now ; along the path
Decay waves sallow arms o'er Autumn lands ;
But in those fields where first we claspèd hands,
Thy face still smiles amid the aftermath,
And cheats my fancy with a dream of Spring.

II.

FROM SHORE TO SHORE.

Sorrow hath built a palace in my soul,
With windows opening on eternity,
And thence I see Time's dreary waves slip by,
Swollen with human tears, and onward roll
To chilling shores of death, their final goal.
Dark burthens on the heaving waters lie,
Tossed to and fro beneath an iron sky ;
Wrecked hopes, wrecked hearts, wrecked lives
  that once were whole.

Poor ships, so soon destroyed by envious waves !
So soon to founder hidden rocks between !
Or else becalmed for aye on arid sand,
Near those dim gardens filled with nameless
  graves,
Wherein we lay to rest what might have been,—
Anchor not here ; there is a Better Land.

III.

HEIGHTS.

THE things that tower above us as we go,
Of their high nature solitary are ;
Spire leaneth not to spire, nor star to star,
Nor even with their peers do angels know
Friendship as felt by lesser hearts below.
And thus some souls will break their human bar,
And o'er their fellow-pilgrims soar afar,
Not from disdain,—but they are framèd so.

What though their lot seem barren, joyless,
        rude—
Let us not pity, we, whose thoughts incline
To shepherd's pipe and cries about the hearth ;
All things are theirs ; new heavens and new
        earth,
New heights, new depths,—the sense of solitude
Makes, in its workings, loneliness divine.

IV.

AFTERWARDS.

LIFE'S darkest hours are not the hours we weep
Prone on the grave of recent happiness ;
The soul's worst pain is when the pain grows
    less,
And Sorrow, wearied, lays h~ down to sleep.
Our highest powers are f.   Ever creep
Time's icicles about our wells of tears ;
Of love and loss, with slow succeeding years,
The narrowed heart may only memories keep.

Father of all ! Who fashionest our dust,
When Thou wouldst heal the heart Thou mak'st
    to bleed,
Forbear ! A greater boon I ask of Thee.
O grant me strength to live, if live I must,
However brief the joys Thou hast decreed,
But let my grief, great God, undying be !

V.

"TONGUES IN TREES."

UPON the time that Autumn hedges wilt,
And monkish weeds the pilgrim year beseem,
When through bereaven woods the thrushes' lilt
Sounds ghostly sweet, like music heard in dream :
Above a road where dying leaves were spilt,
One soaring ash-tree caught the heavenly beam.
And framed in naked branches evening-gilt
The tranquil, vast, illimitable gleam.

When I am old and hoar and like to die,
And hopes and plumed ambitions fall from me,
Might I thus steadfast meet my Father's sight.
Uplifted in a spiritual light ;
That the last fibres of my life might be
A golden lattice to Eternity.

VI.

HIC JACET.

METHOUGHT the earth was fair and sweet and
    green,
Until they pierced it for my true love's grave ;
Then through that narrow door there came a
    wave
Of cold clear light from outside worlds unseen,
And all things changed from what they once had
    been.
How shrunk are their proportions, seeming
    brave !
Yet what they have, and what they claimed to
    have
There lies but one small mound of grass between.

My lady and my love ! sleep'st thou so cold ?
O then have Life and Death exchangèd parts !
Life is a spectre, Death hath all the bloom,
And grows his sweetest flowers under mould.
Here is my only home, beside this tomb,
Whose stony portals now divide our hearts.

VII.

THE URN OF GOD.

ALL things are beautiful and all are great !
God in His world abideth, not alone
In works immortal ; sculptured dreams of stone ;
Music that makes the inner heart vibrate ;
Or moods of nature : seas irradiate ;
Wild branches tossing in a stormy light ;
Winds, waves, bloom, sunrise,—visions exquisite
That human souls to higher spheres translate ;

But lift the humblest daisy from the ground,
And note how wonderful its mimic wheel !
The axle gold, the spokes of rosy white,
The lesser circle in the greater bound ;
Do not its harmony and law reveal
That flower-cups may hold the Infinite ?

VIII.

LASSITUDE.

LIFE'S bonds are countless as its running sands,
Entangling souls with knowledge, love and fame.
How shall we bear each hour's insistent claim,—
Such quick relentless days, such thronged de-
    mands,
Such ceaseless toil for brain and heart and hands,
As duty treads on duty, aim on aim,
Till pulse and impulse stagger in the frame,
Like weary wayfarers in crowded lands !

O it were luxury to pause, reclined
In some lone nook 'mid leafage of the year ;
To shutter close all windows in the mind
And know our loved ones happy, but not near ;
No question forming there, nor finding zest
Nor meaning anywhere, but only rest.

C

IX.

TO A NIGHTINGALE.

MINSTREL unseen, who singest to the skies,
Hope not to make the vestal night pulsate
To such wild strains of music passionate ;
For she on Heaven hath fixed her virgin eyes,
And, deaf to thine entrancing melodies,
Doth quiring angels, silent, contemplate,
While, hid in shadow, thou may'st sing and wait,
To thine own longing making sad replies.

Here is thy love ! O see, at Heaven's edge
Where trees expectant stand along the ridge,
Thy song is crowned ere yet its ardour sinks ;—
Dawn leans her down through golden window-
    bars
And flings with shining hands her wreathèd
    pinks
Among the silver lilies of the stars.

X.

EASTER-DAY.

LET us not dream our loved ones die alone !
We too are straitened in their winding-sheet,
We wear their charnel weeds, our willing feet
Were fain to follow theirs in ways unknown.
We stand o'er graves where yet no grass hath
     grown,
And on ourselves place funeral garlands sweet ;
Something within our hearts hath ceased to
     beat,
Something of us is laid beneath the stone !

And though in time with Christ we rise again,
So changed are we that those who loved us
     most,
And early seek us in God's garden-plot,
Did we not speak to them, would seek in vain,
Like her who, searching for her Saviour lost,
Wept at His piercèd feet, and knew Him not.

XI.

TWO WINDS.

I HAVE within my soul a garden fair
Where twin-born winds dispute the chequered
    skies ;
One dulls the glory on the flower and dries
The roses' dew, and strips the bushes bare,
And broods in darkling bowers, awaking there
Wild dreams of tones long hushed and vanished
    eyes,
Until from grass-grown graves old ghosts arise
And shriek out " Loneliness ! " through empty
    air.

The other softly comes on silver wing,
Beneath whose touch all glamour is renewed,
Once more on swaying boughs and grasses
    spring
Apples of gold and blossoms many-hued,
While through the stillness Angel-voices sing
And dreamy echoes answer, " Solitude."

XII.

ON THE SONNET.

SECURELY through the sonnet's fourteen bars
As from a lattice Poesy looks down ;
While other citadels of song are blown
Into the dust with every wind that wars.
No storms assail her here, no fashion mars ;
Immortal wreaths have round the casement
    grown,
Through which she marks our human smile and
    frown,
Or lifts a pensive gaze to holy stars.

O Poesy ! be ever safe immured
Here, where the mightiest have paused to sing,
And fledgling bards lisped forth their waking
    note ;
And haply to thy cloister-prison lured,
May flights of music stay a wandering wing,
As once of old in Barbara's tower remote.

SIR BION.

SIR BION rode through the Northern land,
His hounds at heel, his hawk on his hand ;
The wild deer crouched in their ferny lair,
The wild doves wheeled in the hot June air,
The wild bee swung on the moor-bell's stalk,
The lark sang loud, and the knight sang low,
As through the thickets he pacèd slow,
But never he loosed his hooded hawk.
'Twixt banks still warm with the may's last flush,
Blossomed and bloomed a syringa-bush ;
Sir Bion caught at a dewy wreath,
And broke it off as he rode beneath ;
Sir Bion a year and a day was wed :—
" Better a wreath for my lady's hair
Than a blood-stained fawn !" Sir Bion said.

The gates were open, the doors unbarred,
The men were scattered in castle-yard,
Upon the stairs stood a woman-throng,
Then came a sad-faced friar along ;

"The Lord remembered thy house this day ;
Thy lady bore thee a son at noon,
A small dead babe in its seventh moon ;
Blest be the will of the Lord, alway !"
Thus prayed the monk, and the women wept ;
A sudden wind through the ivy crept ;
The yew-trees nodding above the wall
Flung passing shadows across them all,
But darkness over Sir Bion shed :
" Better were never a cradle song,
Than a mother's dirge !" Sir Bion said.

The wind rose higher, the branches tossed,
The men turned pale as themselves they
      crossed,
The monk uplifted a face of dread :
"Alas, Sir Bion ! Thy bride is dead !"
They told him the hour she sank to rest,
They told her grief and her gentle prayer,
They bade him clamber the winding stair,
And lay his wreath on her pulseless breast.
Sir Bion heard and he answered not ;
He strode from thence to a silent spot,
A weedy patch called the lych-gate plot,
Where thorn and thistle and nettle plume
O'er ivied ground made a low green gloom,

And there he flung him with heart of lead :
" Better it were had I never wed
Than wedded to weep !" Sir Bion said.

So still he lay that the snails 'gan climb,
And striped his vesture with paths of slime ;
The herbs he bruisèd smelt poison-sweet ;
Then came a weasel to sniff his feet,
And a cloud of wailing gnats drew near.
Sir Bion lay and he heeded naught,
His mind had turned to his battles fought,
And deeds of blood and the foeman's spear.
He thought on war and the corpses grim
Before the walls of Jerusalem ;—
The heaps of slain with their eyes upturned
To skies of brass where a hot sun burned,
And those that fell with a ghastly smile
'Neath his charger's hoofs : and all the while
There tolled a deep-mouthed bell overhead :
" Better my heart should have ceased to beat
Than so heavy lie !" Sir Bion said.

From lonely tracts in the bare wide skies
The stars were staring with alien eyes ;
And through the night by the turret-wing
A white moon past like a hunted thing.

The mastiff dragged at its chain and bayed,
As steps drew nigh in shadow and gloom,
And crept upstairs to the silent room
Where weary watchers slumbered and prayed.
Sir Bion's lady was cold and dead,
With seven tall tapers round her head ;
Seven tall flames that flickered and flared—
But his hand ne'er shook as the blade he bared :
" Better a bier and an earthen bed
And the hand I kissed in its wedding-ring
Than lonely splendour !" Sir Bion said.

The women shrieked and the friars frowned ;
"We may not put him in holy ground."
Up rose the people in dole and wrath ;
" Shall one be flung on the roadside path,
And one be buried in hallowed sod
Whose hands were joined in the Church of God?"
They stood by night on the moorland crest
They brought their tools to the thicket shade ;
Under the bridebush a grave they made,
And laid the knight and his love to rest.
The wild deer crouched in their ferny lair,
The wild doves circled in radiant air,
The wild bee swung on the moor-bell's stalk,
And old and listless grew hound and hawk,

While cowslips sprang from the bride's gold hair,
And spear grass over Sir Bion spread :
" Better together in mould unblest
Than parted in death ! " the people said.

GLAMOUR.

THE wind is blowing from the height,
The hillside gorse has gathered light,
The day is widowed of the sun,
And dies upon a flaming pyre.
Through shifting glories of the sky
The golden argosies sail by,
To reel and founder one by one,
And vanish in a sea of fire.
The air is full of startled wings,
And calling notes, and tossing boughs,
And eerie cries of feathered things,
That heighten as the twilight grows ;
And voices from the solemn seas
Send rustling echoes through the fern,
Where lone upon the lonely leas
A ruin's battered windows burn.

Through loosened tiles the sunset gleams ;
Old cobwebs dangle from the beams ;

The casements rattle ; creepers twine
Green arms about the gabled walls ;
The grass grows lush beside the doors,
And mildew creeps o'er broken floors,
Where blazing trails of Autumn vine
Make chilly fires in roofless halls.
There comes a rustle in the leaves,
The wind swings round the creaking vane.
The jasmine drooping from the eaves,
Beats wildly on the window-pane ;
And where its tendrils interlace
Round ancient glass that fronts the west,
I see a strange and lovely face
Against the glowing lattice prest.

Like Summer lightning in the air,
Its vivid beauty trembles there ;
The shaken rose-bush whispering
Sends forth a sudden breath of musk.
Then swiftly dies the sunset flame,
The vision darkens in its frame,
And flitting shapes on leathern wing
Flash circling through the deepening dusk.
The door swings loudly on its hinge,
My steps are on the crazy stair ;
The echoes start, the shadows cringe,

The owls fly hooting from their lair ;—
I stand within the latticed room,
Where dust and darkness reign supreme,
A cat emerges from the gloom,
And hissing wakes me from my dream.

DETHRONED.

THERE is a warlike music in the blast ;
The rebel winds have risen and discrowned
The aged year, and strewn upon the ground
The gold and crimson of his splendours past.

Poor monarch ! he hath cast his honours down,
Shaken with storms, and pierced with frosty
      spears
Hath fled to sanctuary and now wears
In lieu of kingly state the friar's brown.

Death hath enrolled him in his house of gloom,
Who first stole Summer from the flowering lea,
Nor much I think he cares for life since she
Was laid with all her roses in the tomb.

But now kind Heaven doth avenge his woes,
Confounding those who called him Fortune's
      fool ;
For where he dying lies comes holy Yule
To blanch his memory with saintly snows.

MY KNIGHT, MY DREAM, MY APPLE-TREE.

I HAD a dream at break of day,
When April decked the land with green,
And moated beams and roundelay
Stole in the casement chinks between
To scare the muffled dusk away
With pipes of dawn and light serene.

I dreamed that in a lonely close,
O'er morning grasses long and lush,
I wandered 'neath entangled boughs,
And saw the latticed heavens blush
And brighten all the fruit-tree rows
Above a song of hidden thrush.

And lo ! beside an apple-tree,
With dappled buds and bloom bepearled,
Where docks and nightshade sprouting free
Green tongues about my footsteps curled.

There leaned against the trunk with me,
The fairest knight in all the world.

And as, in dream, my heart beat strong,
And half I thought to turn and flee ;
And louder rose the thrush's song
Above the minor minstrelsy ;
My lover smiled the boughs among,
And kissed me 'neath the apple-tree.

O whence this boding tone, sweet thrush,
In secret coverts overhead ?
The world's a-bloom, the daisies flush,
And all the little birds are wed ;
And Spring on thorn and elder-bush
Hath bridal garlands newly shed,—

O cease thy dagger-note ! The glade
Is pierced with song in every part,
The sun, erewhile in mist arrayed,
Now stabs the leaves with fitful dart ;
And now my knight hath drawn his blade
And plunged it through my trusting heart.

Beneath the nightshade hoar with dew
In haste my maiden grave he spread,

And chilly mould and pebbles threw
Above my murdered golden head,
And down the boughs of apple drew
To make green curtains for my bed.

I would not wake, though to and fro
Long ivy roots bind hand and knee,
But where my lover laid me low
At rest for ever would I be,
And listen while the thrush sings slow
My dirge upon the apple-tree.

D

THE LOST DREAM.

LIKE storm of snow on April maze
Sleep falls upon the darkening mind,
And thoughts are whirled and intertwined
Ere settling down in tangled ways.

The blinding softness numbs the will,
And blurs the edge of memory clear ;
And hooded purposes appear
Like frozen giants cold and still.

From stranger lands beyond the brain
A dream comes through this hushed retreat,
And prints the paths with flying feet,
Then wanders into space again.

And we, with folded senses furled
A fathom deep beneath the snow,
Are dimly conscious then, and know
Her footsteps in the slumber world.

And when at dawn its phantoms melt
To mist about the rising day,
And things of night have fled away,
Her passage through the soul is felt.

Some trifling word or act will fill
Life's thoroughfares with thoughts of her,
And formless memories rise and stir
The baffled heart with sudden thrill.

In vain, in vain we search the spot
Where late the airy pilgrim stood ;
Perchance we meet a sweeter mood,
But our lost dream returneth not.

BESIDE THE SEA.

ALONE beside the radiant seas,
I watched the sun-spears pierce the deep ;
And saw the stealthy shadows creep
Around a mystery of trees.

And in the far-off land of dreams
A fairy hall of pearl I built,
And placed it where the sunset gilt
The rocking tide in lavish streams.

But lo ! Within those waters bright
Both sun and castle found a grave,
Now stand I by the bitter wave
And wait the coming of the night.

TO LILLA.

I.

SHE is dead !
My love is dead !
And nothing earthly hath a meaning now,
Since her sweet spirit fled.
Those who, like me, have laid their dearest low,
And stand alone the hallowed mould above,
May find in memory the things they miss,
And lifting from the dust a lovèd face,
Be happy sometimes for a little while
In the remembrance of a vanished smile,
In echoes of the tender words once said.
But what an added bitterness is this :
I have no past 'twixt me and empty space—
I knew not that I loved my love—
And she is dead !

II.

Last night I dreamed of Heaven ! That I was
    drawn

Beyond the faint carnation fields of dawn,
And through the golden gates to Paradise.

I heard the sound of harps and psalteries ;
I saw the ecstasy of angel eyes ;
I saw innumerable pinions rise
To waft me on to everlasting rest ;—
And yet from this deep bliss I felt estranged,
Nor realised 'twas Heaven, till among
The blessed troops that down in welcome prest,
I caught the sudden silence in thy song,
And saw thy face—and knew thou wert un-
        changed !

III.

This is the thought that will not let me rest
On nights of sob and storm, as still I lie !
For once I dreamed my year-dead love came by,
Out of the wilds with snow upon her head,
And clasped her small soft hands against my
        breast
As was her wont in olden days, and said :
" How cold, dear heart, is great Eternity !"

NESTLINGS.

IN the sweet Spring, in green sweet Spring,
When mist about the morn is spun,
Shot through and through with silver sun,
And chirp perplext of countless birds
Beneath a drowsy sky ;
Ere yet the magic month takes wing,
And days in duller hues are drest,
Shall we not build an April nest,
'Mid blossoms cool and white as curds,
Fancy, the birds, and I ?

Of straws through which the wind pipes free,
And moss that grows by secret streams,
And gossamers as light as dreams,
Our airy dwellings rise to song,
Upon a wilding spray ;
Therein we place our joys to be ;
And some are tinted like the skies,
And others like the loved one's eyes,

Or shells by distant oceans flung
On shores that foam alway.

Then swift ! the brief sweet moon is o'er,
From tender hearts the broods have flown,
Our nests about the hills are blown,
And scattered troops of houseless things
Disperse fresh fields among.
But if in sleep return a few,
To lisp us low the notes we knew,
Shall we not joy that they have wings.
And we have hatched a song ?

SONG.

My love and I went maying when the bloom
    was on the thorn,
High above us larks were singing at the golden
    gates of morn ;
White with blossom lay the meadows, dewy
    fresh the summer lands,
Where I bent the milky branches to her little
    milky hands,
And the sunbeams lingered lovingly to see my
    true love pass,
As her shadow trembled lightly o'er the flower
    of the grass.

O ! my love and I went maying ! but how soon
    her footsteps lagged,
Soon the tender limbs grew weary, and the
    blithesome spirit flagged !
O ! the flowers were very heavy, and the sun
    was fierce on high !

I must pick the rest without her—she would
    meet me by-and-by.
Then she dropped her scented burden in a white
    and shining heap
Near the little hillside churchyard, where she
    laid her down to sleep.

Where my love and I went maying, I came
    down the path alone,
Through the chilly evening thicket while the
    turtle-doves made moan,
With the boughs we broke together closely held
    against my breast,
Though the bloom had long dropped from them,
    and the thorns alone I prest.
And the hawthorn—O ! the hawthorn ! waved
    above me white and red,
But I never more shall pick it, for my little love
    is dead !

SONG.

EVERY star as twilight grows
Nimbly twirls its silver toes ;
Every wind doth set the rose
Dancing on its briar sweet ;
Every heart its gladness knows,
Every lover's heart must beat.
Then it trippeth lightly, lightly,
Lightly as a maiden's feet.

Every twang of Cupid's bows
Singeth out a maiden's name ;
Every dart the urchin throws
Hath a maiden's breast for aim ;
Maidens' eyes make lovers' flame,
Maidens' sighs are lovers' fame,
Therefore, love, come softly, softly,
Softly not to fright the game.

NEW YEAR BELLS.

WHAT say the bells ? Where are last year's joys?
Gone like April flowers that a breath destroys.
Joys are shining pilgrims in a world bereaven :
   With a sound of song
   Come the angel throng,
Pass through our doors and wander on to Heaven.

What say the bells ? Where are last year's woes?
Here, here for ever ; thorns outlive the rose.
In the darkened chambers whence our gladness
  fled,
   Through the lagging days,
   Hooded sorrow stays,
By the cold hearthstone brooding o'er the dead.

What say the bells ? Cast away thy grief,
Let thy future freshen with the springing leaf;
April buds and blossoms shall the graveyard
  strew,

Till the falling blooms,
Covering the tombs,
Make for thy footsteps paths of peace anew.

What say the bells? Heart! in vain, in vain,
Through the drifted blossoms rise the graves
again,
Yet although in loneliness thy weary ways be set,
Faint not, but believe,
Better 'tis to grieve,
Better to grieve, dear heart, than to forget.

CROCUSES.

Nurslings of wind !
Soft crocuses ! what do ye here
Ere buds on currant-bushes sere
With sap are yet incarnadined ?
Ere leaves of ash have slipped their sable hoods
In meads still silvered o'er by wrinkled floods ?

Could ye not patient bide
Till April wandered down the plains among ?
April the bride !
Who cometh veiled in white that mocks the
      fleece
Of February's lambs ;—whose voice is song,
And water murmuring of new release,
There where the mountain streamlet is untied.
Lo ! even now her step is on the hills,
And soon for playfellows come daffodils,
Her golden trumpeters ; soon one by one
Wake the gay birds, and pompously the sun

Like a great cardinal in scarlet state,
With his wild choir doth matins celebrate.

O gentle pilgrims, go not from the field
Where the new season lieth lightly sealed
In horny cradles on the thicket spires ;
Now feather these afresh each spreading plume,
Now runs the sap like wine, and now the briars
Mantle their rougher moods with silken bloom.

O gentle pilgrims, linger and behold
The wild white roses dewily uprolled,
As all-unconscious sweet as infants' dreams ;
Linger and hear the blackbird's song of ruth,
Linger and see the daisy-tide that seems
The laughter of the meadows in their youth.

No, no, alas ! I pipe, I pipe in vain.
I see ye will not stay
To grace with vestal lamp the marriage train,
Upon the nuptial day.
Fair prophets ! who have borne the storm and
      smart, I
Preaching sweet light and warmth when all was
      chill,
Now fare ye well, for hence ye must depart,
Ere your bright promises themselves fulfil.

OLYMPUS IN BABYLON.

COME, wandering Poet, leave the hills behind ;
The gods are dead ; thou canst not wake them
    more.
No more will Hebe blush or Dian wind
Her silver horn upon the forest floor.
Pipe as thou wilt, thou may'st not reach the
    strain
That braced Minerva's virgin arm with might,
And throbbed to thund'rous clashings of the
    forge
Where limping Vulcan and his Cyclop train
Hammered in shadow of their mountain gorge
To arm the hero of Homeric fight.

Wouldst thou for ever waste a tuneful breath
Wooing an echo now austerely mute?
Leave, Poet, leave the mighty ones in death,
And to an earthlier music pitch thy lute.
The gods are dead ! What then? Shall men
    forget

To love, to hate, to combat, and to weep?
No, no, though old Olympus' sun be set
Its many springs of deathless passion roll
Through all humanity, and still we keep
These primal powers and Titans of the soul !

Here by the stormy tides that ebb and flow
About the lives of men, build thou thy art ;
Beat out thy lay, nor deem the key too low
That tunes with voices of the human heart.
The grace, the strength, the splendour that we
      crave
Lie ever hid these moving deeps among ;
Be thine the task from daily foam and drift
New shapes divine, new glory to uplift,
Like Aphrodite from the morning wave,
In perfect loveliness of truthful song.

E

FAIRY SONG.

WHEN daisies close and poppies nod,
And meadow grass to earth is laid,
And fairies dance on moonlit sod,
Or quaff of dewdrops in the shade,
Come ! gentle dreams, in velvet shod,
And foot it round each sleeping maid.

Come softly hither, dove-winged flock,
And on their pillows make your nest,
And light as down from puff-ball clock
Let kisses on their eyes be prest,
Then sit upon the couch and rock
Each tender little heart to rest.

AT SUNDOWN.

O TENDRIL of ivy and tangle of tree,
Wild are the banks of my ain countrie !
The sun is sinking low in the west,
A golden ball o'er the mountain crest ;
 Shafts of light pierce the moorland's breast.
Wild are the banks of my ain countrie.

O purple of heather and silver of sea,
Bright are the hues of my ain countrie !
A fairy knight rides out of the wold,
A lady's sleeve round his helm is rolled ;
His coal-black charger is shod with gold.
Bright are the hues in my ain countrie.

O ripple of streamlet and murmur of bee,
Sweet are the sounds in my ain countrie !
He throws me, passing, a glance remote ;
A wandering lark in the clouds afloat
Hath stabbed my soul with its tender note.
Sweet are the sounds in my ain countrie.

O shadow of pine-wood and silence of lea,
Cold falls the dew in my ain countrie!
The love-light fades in the amber sky
And grey mists over the forest fly ;
We are alone, my heart and I.
Cold falls the dew in my ain countrie.

THE SILENT KNIGHT.

OCTOBER days, frail daughters of the sun,
O'erweighted by the pomp of royal state,
Early decline and darken to their death.
For earth luxurious grown through glut of gold,
Sated with splendour, riotous and rich,
With reckless pageant fills a lawless court,
And flings her treasures broadcast to the wind ;
Nor dreams the wintry foe is at her gate
Till warned of Heaven, whose avenging hand,—
Which once in halls of gorgeous wickedness
Wrote *Mene, Tekel, Phares*, on the walls,
Striking cold terror and confusion there,—
Now, in the night, on every leaf and blade
With frosty finger writes its doom in rime.

I was a pilgrim once in sylvan ways,
'Neath skies as blue as June, and yet I knew
The Autumn world was in its agony.

The sweat of death lay heavy on the grass,
And damp and limp hung ferns along the hedge ;
Leaves fluttered slowly down in amber drifts,
Or else like curved and crumpled golden shells
Lay strewn about the path, from ebbing tides
Of Summer beauty washed on Winter's shore.
And where the level sun glanced through the
    trees,
Fringing with glory and ethereal light
Their ragged boughs, and all the forest shone
Transfigured in the pure embrace of Heaven,
In a green spot remote I lit upon
An ancient church, that solitary rose
Above the crowded loneliness of graves.
The door was open ; nothing stirred within
Save floating stains of dim magnificence
From the great windows framed in moving
    leaves,
And which, like radiant shades of vanished
    saints,
Hovered about the ruins of their shrines.
Chill was the air as of that colder age
Which quenched the sacred fire in the land,
And from the ashes of forbidden rites
Proffered dry prayers to a far-distant God.
But carven glories of a banished faith

Still lingered brokenly round empty niche,
And down the shadowy aisles ; and o'er the dead
Immortal garlands kept a hoary Spring
Of leaf and bud, where, prone above their tombs
A race of knights for ever slept in stone.
A line of warrior princes, sires and sons,
Each in his armour with his shield on arm,
His sword beside engraven with his name ;
And at the end of all, where most the light
Through lancet panes a moated radiance cast,
The marble figure of a maiden stood,
Slender upon its massive pedestal.
Beneath was carven deep a name, a date,
The one word "*Silence*" in the Latin tongue,
And nothing more. But he whose hand had
          made
Of pulseless stone the loveliest thing on earth,
A lovely woman, through its earthly veils
Of fold, and form, and face, and rippling hair,
Had caught the music of the soul within
And trammelled it in marble, and it shone
A spiritual presence, silver-white,
Placed like a wingless angel o'er the dead.

Strange contradictions of the grave were here !
Grim satires on the lives now past away !

These stalwart knights who loved to fight and
    feast,
Nor often let the abbey walls resound
To the bright music of their clinking steel,
Reformed by death, now prayed eternally,
With hands devoutly joined, and mailèd feet
Upon th' ancestral lion stiffly placed !
And she, the virgin daughter of the house,
Who best mid convent lilies might have lived,
Faded with them, and laid her vestal form
In its last slumbers 'neath their drifted blooms,
Nor habit wore, nor cross, nor heavy coif,
Such as beseem the spouses of the Lord,
But simplest robes, and o'er her guileless face
Beauty's best veil, the veil of mystery.
Lo ! she of all the mighty ones at rest
Would silence counsel, yet alone did speak ;
And mute perchance in life, when ruder tones
Of kinsmen echoed round her, had in death
A voice to bridge the chasm of years wherein
They and their noisy deeds engulfèd lay !

The heavens flamed and paled ; the twilight
    hour
Descended with the dew on humbler graves
Without the porch.   I left the church and paced

Among the ruined monastery walls,
Where beaded flowers wept about my feet
In ways of death, and chilly scents arose
As of an Autumn garden, coldly sweet ;
In boughs of yew a tender robin piped
Its sad insistent song ; all else was hushed.
It was a windy evening, and the grass
Stirred on the graves as though long-quiet hearts
Began to beat within ; the present hour
Faded away, and shadows of the past
Mingled with those now creeping o'er the
      mounds.
And I struck out a path across the fields,
While silver stars came trembling forth in turn
Through orange rifts of sky above the hills ;
But not alone I walked, for phantom forms
And one fair ghost of peerless loveliness
Hovered beside me : and I reached the inn,
The old-world inn where old tradition held
Time-honoured court beneath a gabled roof,
With beating heart and all my brain on fire
To learn the legend of the marble maid.

Simplicita, the last of all her race,
The last pale blossom on the hoary thorn,
Far from her father's court to holy walls

Was brought one Summer's morn, a fragile babe
Too early motherless.   And there the nuns
Received her lovingly as God's own gift,
And, mid a thousand prayers of purest lips
Breathed hourly to the Lord, the flickering life
Shot up a steady flame and sweetly glowed
Round hearts that had maternity forsworn.
Unconscious of her orphaned state, the child
Waxed strong and beautiful, and daily ran
With pattering feet among the sisterhood,
From choir to hall, from hall to garden-ways,
Nor needed playfellows, but on the walls
Traced elfin faces in discoloured cracks,
And found in each familiar tree a friend ;
Loved hound, and flock, and fowl, and oft, while
        yet
A little tumbling thing whose small bright head
Scarce reached the lowest bud on lily stems,
Would pause from play in cloistered squares to
        watch
The convent doves, as high against the blue
They wheeled, the light upon their breasts, and
        beat
With shadow-coloured wings the golden air.
Then, all in ecstasy, the little maid,
Waving small arms in impotent desire,

Would dance and caper on the paven court,
And ape their feathered joys and long for
      wings :—
So sweet a vision that her keepers deemed
The grimmest gargoyle on the ancient roof
Had lion jaws wide spread to smile on her !
Later, when childish freedom was exchanged
For early tasks and manners more sedate,
Her joy was unperceived to slip away
Alone, through abbey woods and meadow-lands,
And watch in Spring the painted finches flit
Round their small nest embosomed in the thorn ;
Or breathe the woodbine's incense as it drooped
Its antlered head above a noontide pool ;
To the mild summons of the vesper bell
Returning from her rambles erst at eve,
Blooming and fearless ; for the gentle nuns
Forbore to chide their truant, knowing well
That sights and sounds of nature sinking deep
In souls unconscious, leave their freshness there,
And lend to youth an added youthfulness.

So passed the lengthy sheltered years away,
Clustered about with tearful hopes and prayers
As thick as dewy leaves around a nest.
And evermore her aunt, the Abbess, strove

To fit the girl for splendid cares to come ;
And daily sought to cram the fledgling mind
With such sound knowledge as beseemed her
        rank.
But she, as much as in her nature lay,
Loathed the mock blossoms in her tapestry,
And poring on the convent's crabbèd books
Stumbled o'er letters, shedding countless tears,
And held them dark and dwarfish foes to joy.
Thus, although docile, dutiful, and sweet,
And humbly anxious her good aunt to please,
Simplicita with learning strove in vain ;
And those, who fain around her young mind's
        dawn
Had painted their own hopes in glowing tints,
Saw with misgiving as it broadened out,
Faint vapours clouding o'er the perfect light,
And blankly felt the day was colourless.
Yet none the less, her innocence of heart
Shed its own halo round her looks serene ;
And now though turning seasons brought her
        height
And stately bearing, ever on her brow
Shone out the look that mothers love in babes
When soft they say, "The angels speak with
        them !"

Seventeen years had passed and it was Spring,
Spring, and the convent rooks began to dream
Of sable broods among the budding elms
Outside the Abbess' cell. The Abbess slept
After a long day's work, oppressed with years
And toil and prayer, when of a sudden rose
A gale without, and though it woke her not,
She dimly heard the storm-bird's voice and
          knew
The buffet of its pinions on the panes.
And all her mind made war with dreadful shapes ;
Wild dreams in phantom ships that ride by night
Upon the formless billows of the wind,
And, wrecked upon our pillows, cast their freight
Of fears chaotic through the helpless brain.
Then she bethought her of the building rooks
And pitied them, and seemed to see them dashed
From writhing trees above their shattered nests ;
And as she gazed, behold ! they were not rooks,
But eagles hovering fierce about a lamb—
A white ewe-lamb that bleated not, nor stirred ;
And then a time of darkness came and lo !
The child of her old age, Simplicita,
Entered her dream and stood beside the couch,
One taper finger resting on her lips,
And on her face the doubtful, piteous smile

That little children wear when angry tones
Scare them from play, and all perplext they
    stand,
With trembling hearts, unconscious of their fault.
Fain had the Abbess roused her then to speak,
And stretch out loving arms, but could not move;
And as she struggled, downward bent the maid
And whispered " Silence."

               With the word she woke
To feel her tower rocking in the gale;
But over and above the sounds of storm,
The cawing rooks and gusts of driving rain,
Heard a loud knocking at the convent gates,
And her heart knew it was its knell of doom.
Trembling she rose and met the frightened nuns,
Scattered like sheep unpenned about their cells;
While ever louder trampling hoofs and steps·
Of heavy feet in vaulted ways of stone
Woke unaccustomed echoes in the place,
And the rude message came from those below:
" The prince is dead : deliver up the girl,
For she must sit upon her father's throne,
And hold his realm against the foe without !"
O then came long embraces, clinging, tears;
Last words half choked of counsel, comfort, hope;

A flash of torches, armour gleaming out,
Retreating steps, and all was emptiness.
And the dawn breaking shone on splintered
      boughs,
Torn nests, and on the vacant stall in choir,
Near which the aged Abbess knelt and raised
Above the bowed and weeping sisterhood
A voice scarce audible for years and grief:
" O God ! who givest and who takest away,
Keep Thou our lamb unspotted from the world!"

Weeks passed ; then came a rumour from the
      court,
A poisoned shaft to pierce the convent walls,
The noble maid was well, but sad of mien,
Nor loved the pageants made to welcome her.
The knights and barons murmured, and rebelled
At bending stubborn heads before a nun,
Or so they called her!—then came cautious
      hints
Concerning one, a kinsman of the prince,
In touch with all the nobles, and whom some
Had fain seen lord of what his cousin left.
Quarrels were rife. One scarce could blame the
      girl ;
Belike she still was mourning for the prince.

So much the Abbess with misgiving heard,
Knowing the child, however dutiful,
Had never felt nor missed a father's love ;
And fearing worse things for Simplicita,
And war and bloodshed in the land through her,
Crushed down the yearning mother in her heart
And sent a missive by a trusty squire,
Bearing on duty ; couched in bracing terms,
Herself from duty too forbore to speak
One over tender word, nor laid her bare
The wound still raw and smarting for her loss.

The letter reached Simplicita at eve,
Within the summer palace as she sate
High in her bower, above the noisy hall,
And lonely, for her women were at meat ;
And what it said and what it left unsaid
Struck daggerwise on her bewildered soul.
A coarser beauty and a stouter heart
Had carried all before them ; or had hers
Been of those natures light as thistledown,
Whose chiefest charm is that they care to charm,
Yet careless are of what they most have charmed,
She might have held grave wisdom's self in thrall,
Chained to the movements of capricious brows.
But ever lowly, diffident of self,

The half-concealed contempt of those around
Crushed her meek life ; she lacked the skill to
    mend,
Grew daily more perplext, and scared, and sad :
And the word "witless" passed from mouth to
    mouth.
One joy she had ; the people worshipped her,
Won by her beauty and her gentle ways,
No less than by the free largesse she gave,
Her poorer vassals loved her, and would throng
About her palfrey as she rode to church,
Kissing her garments, hanging on her smiles ;
This was in truth her only happiness.
Yet since dissensions in the land had risen,
Voices from every class rose up to urge
That she should wed her kinsman, and so drown
With bridal bells the noisy brawls.   But she,
Loathing the name of marriage and the man
(Who led a riotous life nor cared for her,
But fain had filled his coffers with her gold,)
Pleaded her youth, her father's death, and gave
Evasive answers, thinking in her heart
Soon to contrive a meeting with her aunt,
From whose wise counselling she hoped to learn
How best the people to conciliate,
And please the court, yet live and die a maid.

F

Now came the missive brimmed with words of
    weight :
The life of princes lies 'twixt realm and God !
So far as Heaven allows they must in all
Their subjects' wishes meet, though this involve
The utmost sacrifice of self.   The maid
Must convent ways forget and learn to rule,
And where experience failed her, take advice
Of those great lords and learned counsellors
Who had her father's ear in days gone by.

So wrote the Abbess, and the nuns to choir
Trooping at eventide, ere yet the stars
Lit their faint tapers round the young dead day,
Prayed all good angels guard Simplicita,
Whom, in their dreams of things to come, they saw
Enthroned on high amid a glittering court,
The blameless ruler of a happy realm,
And joined in time to some great prince and
    kind,
Beneath whose care their drooping convent bud
Might blossom into rosier womanhood.
O had their eyes been opened to the truth,
How had these simple hearts been torn with
    grief !
How had the loving Abbess wept to see,

Within a turret chamber leagues away,
Her letter lying on the rush-strewn floor,
Blurred with despair ; and in a heap beside
The broidered veil, rich clasps, and strings of
    gems
With which when first she doffed her convent
    garb
Obsequious dames had 'tired Simplicita ;
While down the twilight stair there past, unseen
Of those who sang and supped in hall, the maid,
Lady of all, and flying from wealth abhorred !

II.

In forest ways without, where tangled leaves
Made ebon tracery upon the sky,
And, from the sunset, monstrous cloudy shapes,
With streaming hair and manes, held fiery sport,
Brightening and darkening round the windy
    hills,
The palace jester all in pied attire
Sate on a bough amid the sprouting fern,
Sick of enforcèd revelry in hall.
The dusky air was full of notes and wings,
Dim dewy leaves, and scent of springing grass,
And now and then a stealthy footfall told
Of wild and furry woodland things at large

Roaming the thickets in the doubtful light.
A hare sprang past and then a fawn drew nigh,
Testing the air with graceful head alert ;
Then something paler glimmered in the copse ;
"'Tis a white doe," quoth Alaric, the fool,
"Yet no,—by Venus' doves ! it is a maid—
'Tis royalty herself ! Why, how is this?—
Most noble lady, have ye lost your way?
Let me attend ye home ; the night grows late."
"O fool ! delay me not, I have no home,"
Simplicita replied.   "Let others nest
In what was aye too high a perch for me.
Since the bright heaven of my youth hath closed
Its holy gates, I wander to my grave.
In truth, good jester, I am like the lark,
That knows no resting-place 'twixt sky and sod,
The crown was over heavy for my head,
The lands too wide for me ! So I may find
Six feet of earth in which to lie at peace
I shall be queen enow, nor want a realm."
"Tut, tut," quoth Alaric, "what whim is this?
Death and thy youthful bloom were sore ill-
    matched.
O take a rosier view of life, sweet maid !
Or if alone, thy courage fail thee now,
Bethink thee of thy noble kinsman's suit.

Rough diamond as he is, give him thy hand ;
'Tis hard to judge the finest gem unset,
And near thine eyes perchance he might reflect
A purer beam. Ay, give thy hand, thy heart,
For, lady, know the measure of the joy
We have in others lies within ourselves ;
They are not great, nor wise, nor good, nor true
But as we represent them to our minds ;
Of our own riches do we crown them kings
When once we love ; the will to love is all,
And brings all attributes to grace its train.
True love resembles heaven which we see
Glass its own depth in every shallow pool
And braid the hollow rushes there with stars."
Then said Simplicita : "Ay, gentle fool,
So that the pool be calm, not passion stirred,
Nor spread with evil growth from weeds below,
Else were the golden heavens all unseen,
Or made to shudder in its troubled depths.
But how if that which thou art pleased to call
By the high name of heaven were itself
Obscured with cloud ?—then were a double night
Worn on the sky, and mirrored in the pool !
O mock me not with words—I have had dreams—
But never yet of love ; 'tis not for me,
Whose wits have all these years in darkness lain,

Since ere my birth a cold and adverse wind
Gathered dull vapours round my helpless fate."
" Ay," said the fool, " the coldest wind of all,
Blown from the grave.   I knew thy mother well !
The wisest of the wise ;—her mind a blade
Keen, but the finer edge the sooner turned,
And so 'twas blunted on thy brother's bier,
When home they brought him stark and stiff to
        hall.
And thou, poor innocent, wert born in grief.
Yet mark me this, Simplicita ! 'Tis not
The deepest lore that makes the fullest bliss ;
Hast thou less joy to see the daisy wear,
At dawn and sunset, colours of the skies
Upon its folded blossoms, and at noon
Expand a mimic sun on every mead
Because thou art unlearnèd in its parts ?
Would greater knowledge see a brighter disk ?
Doth it not shine for fool and sage alike ?
O be not over wise, Simplicita,
Perchance a sudden flash athwart the clouds
Might darken all thy tender heart with death.
Eternal Wisdom shaping perfect man
For perfect happiness in Eden gave
All things unto his hand, but one withheld—
Knowledge ; for it and happiness are foes.

Look you, most noble maid, when first man ate
Of fruit forbidden in the dawning world
He reared himself between the virgin earth
And God's great light just risen on the race ;
And ever as he travels to his grave
His shadow falls before him, so that all
Upon his path is darkened with himself
And all distorted in his vision lies.
O, 'tis an everlasting jest ! 'twould make
The laughter of the angels, could they laugh,
To see how we, in vain pursuit of that
Which God withholds us evermore, invent
New gods, new laws, new systems, new beliefs
To suit our fallen powers ; and of these
What doth Time teach? Their folly, nothing
      more.
For we are fools.   From having learnt too much,
We know too little now ; and we are fools,
And make the things we see our folly share ;
Earth, sky, and spheres.   Call you the heavens
      wise ?
The foolish round-faced moon that endless turns
About a giddy world, and wears for all,
Pig-stye and palace, fair and foul alike,
The same unmeaning smile.   Behold the stars,
That see the evil deeds of men and wink !

Had they true wisdom they might hurl themselves
From heaven's vault upon th' offending earth
Till it were purged in flame ! O ay ! the stars !
Or they are fools, or they are over-wise ;
Perchance through nightly watching o'er the race
They learn what men call wisdom, and refrain
From such just vengeance, fearing did they fall
In punishment on what were best unseen,
They might not easily regain their place ;
This is, we know, the wisdom of the great."
   "Peace ! peace ! I pray thee," said the lady
      then ;
" Bend, an thou wilt, the things of mother earth
To fit the lowly passage to my wits,
But lay not hands on heaven's majesty,
Wherein my sick soul's only comfort lies.
O, fool, its loftiness o'ertops our thoughts
Even as its dome the highest mountain peak !
The moon, celestial maid, brings looks serene
To bear upon our weakness ; her pure eyes
Expel the fiend of darkness where they fall,
Nor may she from corruption take alloy.
The shield of innocence is innocence
And fair reflects all foulness.   And the stars !
The human stars that beat like living hearts
Deep in the bosom of the cold blue night ;

Methinks they once in mother breasts did burn
On earth below, and now, though drawn to God,
Their yearning passion for us keeps them poised
On the extremest confines of their bliss,
To throb with every throe of orphans left.
Jester, methinks, for all my mind is dark,
Had my sweet mother lived, she would have
　　loved me !"

Then groaned the fool and springing to his feet
Woke all the dusk with jangling bells, and cried:
"Thine be all love, and thine is wisdom too !
Forgive thy fool, twice fool in that he strove
By jest ill suited to the hour and theme
To lift thy heavy mood to one of smiles.
O leave thy lonely purpose and the paths
Of night and danger in the forest here,
And let to-morrow find thee still a queen.
Methinks thy singleness of heart should bind
The splintered factions to a perfect whole."

Then sighed the maid, "Alas ! good Alaric !
More like their ruggedness would pierce my
　　heart
Until it bled to death.　O stay me not,
I have more terror of enforcèd law
Than of the lawlessness of forest ways.
See how the climbing trees march up the hill,

And how the hills press onward to the sea,
And nodding branches beckon from the wood !
All nature calls me and I follow her.
Ask me not where.   Myself, I know not where
In truth I care not, so I may forget
The world and all its woes.   Farewell, good fool."
    And then the jester, hoping against hope
To keep her there till some should come from
          court,
Armed with authority to break her scheme,
And force her back to palace, cried in haste :
" Tarry awhile, sweet lady ! I have felt
Like thee the glamour of the woods, O ay !
Thy mother felt it too, and mid the toil
And tedium of the court, she used to watch
The summer landscape from her bower, and sing
Sweet stanzas, all on peaceful fields and leaves
And sliding waters, to refresh her soul.
While I behind her gilded chair would crouch,
And hold my breath for fear these foolish bells
Might break upon her dreams.   How does it go,
The song she sang ? the song of lonely land ?
O tarry yet ; I do remember me.

    " I know a land, a lonely land,
    Where green the clustered branches grow,

And o'er a wild and rocky strand,
Enchanted rivers foam and flow.

"There shine and shadow all the day
Creep dreamily athwart the wood,
And faint in far-off caverns play
The magic pipes of solitude.

" There sleeps the troutlet 'neath his stone
In waters golden-brown and cool ;
And bubbles bursting find a tone
To break the silence of the pool.

" When sunset flames the flood beside,
Adown a path of dappled gold
Come troops of deer at eventide,
And pause to drink its waters cold ;

" About the shining waves they lag,
Then through the thickets bound and go ;
To every tree a stately stag
To every stag a milk-white doe . . .

" Most noble lady ! do ye like my song ? "
" I like it well," said sweet Simplicita.

I trust no harm befell the gentle deer?"
"Nay," said the fool, "hear on; the end is best.

"There is a prince in lonely land!
His glance is like the sword of light
That smites the boles on either hand,
In wooded alleys ere the night;

"When outer boughs of pine appear
Like galleries of woven fire,
And wizard glory gilds the mere,
And makes each reed a glancing spire.

"And wheresoe'er his look hath wrought,
A thousand deep enchantments rise,
And simplest things of earth are fraught
With wonder from his mystic eyes.

"And some have seen his armour white,
And blindly tracked the wandering gleam,
And lost, and called him phantom knight,
And all his kingdom but a dream;

"O Prince! O Light! the pure of heart
For ever in thine eyes rejoice;
But none may ask thee whence thou art,
And none hath ever heard thy voice."

"Then an I meet him, fool, I will not speak,"
The maiden said, and with these words she
    smiled
So sweetly, that the jester stared and thought
On the cold tenderness of angel heads,
Whose sculptured eyes behold their hidden
    God
Through veils of stone and tabernacle doors.
And saying once again, "I will not speak!"
She waved her hand, and down the silver gleam
That sped along the grasses slipt away;
While he, with sad foreboding at his heart,
Turned slowly homeward through the trees; nor
    dared
To follow her, but lingered on the way,
And sang at intervals that she might know,
If her heart failed her, that he still was near.

"O love, when wilt thou come?" the jester sang,
"Wilt come in song, the leaves among, with
    April's tender light,
When topmost boughs of apple-trees are flushed
    with young delight;
With yearning buds and bleat of lambs amid the
    daisies white,

Where Spring's warm waves have stirred and
    swelled and burst their frost-bound home,
And dyed the trees and hedges green, and left
    the fields in foam.

" O love, I pray thee, tarry not, for swift the
    seasons go,
Swift melteth from the hawthorn bush its weight
    of scented snow,
Swift purple-hooded Winter stands where now
    the jonquils blow ;
O come while yet the meadows slope in blossom
    to the sea ;
Upon the threshold of the year I pause and wait
    for thee."

High rose his song above the nightingales',
And stilled their ecstasy in hidden bowers ;
And faintly too it reached Simplicita,
And made an answering music in her heart,
Down the wild glen, the home of rushing winds
And out into the wilder woods beyond.

III.

Slow move the jewelled hours across the sky,
While sunk in dreams on pillows dull we lie,

Or mock their flight with lighted dance and song ;
But they, disdainful of the world below,
Its puny revels and unseeing eyes,
Nobly severe, do stately measures tread
With Time upon the azure floors of heaven.
The glorious firmament is ever young,
And bears its æons lightly as its stars ;
From age to age the galaxies lie strewn
Like drifted blossoms of the tree of life
Upon celestial plains ; from age to age
With argent pomp the heavens celebrate
Eternal bridals of the night and moon ;—
When Night in majesty descending slow
Smoothes his dark brows to greet the awakening
    Moon,
And she, upon the brink of deeps unknown,
Trembles a moment, then serenely moves
To meet him, riding on the buoyant airs.
And she is faithful to her swarthy spouse,
But womanlike hath various moods, and times
Turns half a scornful loveliness away,
On solitary musings bent, and times
Hides all with lawny veils of light caprice
Which she calls modesty, nor will unmask
Altho' he woo her with a thousand stars.
But when September ripens through the land,

And the still year is burthened with its fruit,
Then she, forgetful of her vapours, hangs
Full hearted and with matron majesty
Low o'er the fields that wear her liveries gold.
And Night rejoicing in her timely smiles
Makes her the Queen of gorgeous tournaments
Where herald breezes call his shadows forth
Trembling from sheaves and leafy fastnesses,
Predoomed in swift defeat to shrink and fly
Before the shining spearmen of the moon.

Midnight had come and gone upon the world,
The thickets swayed in sleep and mystery
Trailed silken garments lightly o'er the grass.
It was the hour when moonlight, water, dew
Breathe dim romance, and every little leaf
That flutters to his fellow on the bough,
Doth lisp of magic to the poet's ear.
Among the flowers lay Simplicita,
Folded upon herself, with overhead
A hundred years of oak.   And there her soul
Went slipping down white falls precipitous
Of sleep, like sliding snows that evermore
Struck and were shivered on a jutting thought
Of sharp-recurrent woe.   But as the night
Wore on to dawn, from weariness of tears

Came rest and deeper slumbers and a dream.
Lo ! through the seals of sleep, she felt a sigh
Of coming change creep o'er the muffled world,
And heard low notes of waking birds that seemed
To paint the dusk with little shafts of flame.
And out of space about her came a field
Of tulips blowing, streaked with fire, and then
A sound of golden trumpets ringing out,
And noise of arms and trampling horse, and
    sense
Of gorgeous pageant yet invisible ;—   .
And as she struggled towards this burst of life,
Appeared the palace fool and laid his hands
Across her eyes, with warning shriek: "Forbear !
Be wise and look not, lest a sudden flash
Darken thy tender heart with death !" But she,
Impatient, freed her, and the fancied act
Dissolved the drifting glamour of her thoughts
And changed their current ;—now, it seemed,
    she stood
Within the nunnery church whose pillared height
Waved mistily like boughs, and overhead
A mighty window gloomed and glanced, whereon,
Set round with dancing leaves, a mailèd form
Majestic, like a warrior angel, stood,
In feature sternly beautiful. No sword

G

Which brighter grew with ever brightening
    day,
More pallid clear, more nobly beautiful,
Till her own soul mysteriously did seem
To mirror back its deep felicity.
In life our greatest joys deny us peace !
We are so tempered that this edge of bliss
But cuts the furrow of our future tears.
Our joys are keen for that they daggers hold
To stab us unawares ; and all the while
We clasp them close in welcome, traitors ! they
Are whetting stealthy blades upon our hearts.
Yet ere the stroke descends we see it gleam ;
This is the flash men call presentiment !
But naught of fear assailed Simplicita,
Nor cast a shadow o'er untravelled ways.
Bliss all impersonal was hers ; the sky
The beggar's roof and king's ; the placid earth
New-burgeoning, and music in the boughs :—
Nature most lovely, most familiar things
Through avenues of sense her spirit reached,
And steeped and strengthened it, and made it
    glad.

Spring had been busy in the night and built
Her blushing towers on grey-beard apple-trees,

And spread the thorny brakes with primrose
    snares
To net the poet's numbers unawares.
Here o'er deep pits where Winter hid him yet,
A lorn and hunted wight, the young May-month
Gazed shyly forth through violet eyes divine ;
Here cast in sport her rosy aureole down
On ragged robin's beggar brows ; and here,
Where lady-smocks the banks ensheeted fair,
She played at death beneath a maiden pall,
Like nuns when first they make their holy vows.
Anon Simplicita would break a bough,
Foam-white and sparkling as a wavelet's crest,
From wilding plum or cherry-tree ; anon
A linnet from the bloom escaping shook
A glittering shower on her golden hair ;
The birds sang sweetly to her as she passed,
The squirrel shunned her not ; the snake that lay
Like streak of molten ore upon the stones
Slipped not away, but raised a wistful head
In welcome ; shy and downy-coated things
Crept from their lairs to frolic round her steps,
And filled the glades with curious lisping notes,
Ripple of wings, and small incautious feet
Free-pattering through last year's leaves and
    moss

And by and by they left the woods and stood
In meads without, and saw a grassy land
Slope downwards to the sea, and on the grass
Were herds enaureoled in their own sweet breath,
Couchant or grazing, and unnumbered flocks ;—
Here 'neath a thorn they paused, and all was
     peace
From the small innocencies of the field
Nodding their foolish heads o'er daisy tufts,
To the horizon's edge where cloudlets lay
Like other little weary lambs at rest ;—
Yea, from a sweep of laughing ruffled seas
Whence rose new lambs to meet them—merry
     flocks
That topped the hillocks of the watery plain
To fall again within its moving dells ;—
The cadenced song of shoreward creeping tides
Heightened the dream it made believe to break.
It seemed a thousand years since early dawn,
So far the world of yesternight ; so fair
The present and Simplicita's own heart !
And yet the sun was scarcely high in heaven
When o'er the hills there came a bugle call,
By distance thinned to voice of pining gnat,
But gathering strength betimes, and all at once
A sound of trumpets scared the browsing kine

And sent them flying, and the quiet fields
Shook to the thunder of a thousand hoofs.

IV.

Custom ! thou dull and envious wight, who art
Inured to ugliness, to beauty blind,
And hangest on the skirts of Novelty
To trip his rapid steps and cast him down !
Sworn foe to young Enthusiasm ! with hand
And iron sceptre ever raised to blunt
The edge of life, and level all things flat,
To one long, dreary, blank monotony !
Thou—even thou ! hadst days of pomp and fire,
Long past, but once with Valour and with Fame
Didst wander eager-eyed and call them friends ;
Clothe thee in clashing steel ; aye, even now
Up these tame years thy trumpets echo still,
Thy pennons wave, thy legions fearless move
And call them blest to die for God, for King,
For Honour, and their lady's will ;—but then
Thou wert yet vassal unto Chivalry !

Might we have known those golden days and
        stood
'Mid old world meadows with Simplicita,
When fearful of discovery she slipped

Into an elder copse beside the way,
And saw a host of gallant riders pour
Along the levels green, to tournament.
Throng after throng they came ; a glittering
    stream
Bristling with spears as harbour-tides with
    masts ;
Such martial bearing ! and such faces !— some
Aflame with hope, and others ardent pale,
Like those at eve on painted windows seen ;
A noble thirst for glory writ on all !—
And none beheld the maiden as they wound
Past her in line, with scarves and bannerets gay,
Like beds of tulips tinted, and the light
From every spearhead striking shafts of fire.
But young and happy laughter floated back
And vaguely troubled her, and vext her mind
With haunting memories it failed to grasp.
And as, forgetful of all else, she moved
Nearer the path, and watched with dreamy
    eyes
This gust of life sweep through the wilderness,
A knight belated galloped up in haste,
But, spying a fair face 'mid the boughs, drew
    rein
To give her greeting :

"Gentle maid," he said,
" For gentle are ye, surely, tho' ye seem
So wan, so wistful, and with vesture torn,
In straits ill suiting one of lineage high !—
How come ye thus forlorn in this lone land?
Command my services, for they are yours.
And though my lady waits to see me tilt
In yonder stranger city on the plains ;
And though with all my soul and strength I long
For love's dear sake and glory's there to win ;
Yet do I hold it nobler to forego
Such noisy triumph, if by yielding help
To any hapless damsel in distress
I prove myself, perchance, the worthier knight."
" My thanks, fair sir," Simplicita replied.
" But I am not alone, nor in distress.
My state is of my choosing ; and the world
Through all its happy leagues this happy day
Holds not methinks a happier maid than I."
Thereat the knight smiled courteously, and part
To let his panting horse draw breath, and part
To ease his mind of what lay uppermost,
He made his good steed stand, and spake again :
" Are ye so happy? Is the world so fair?
O then, sweet lady, I will read your heart
By what is written in mine own. Ye love

And him ye love, loves back, and when 'tis so
All things seem rosy in love's rosy light.
And I will swear that when ye stole to tryst,
As I perceive ye did in these wild woods,
Ye felt no thorn o'erhead, nor stone afoot
For joy in meeting there your own true knight ! "
" Not so ! " Simplicita exclaimed, " Sir knight,
Such things as these ye name are not for me ! "
" O ay ! " he said and laughed, " Maids ever say
' Not so ! 'tis false,' and think therewith to draw
Shy hangings 'twixt their eyes and timid hearts.
But men may speak the truth, and this is truth ;
Of our own temper do we paint the world
Which else were barren sand and leaf and blade.
And therefore every little bird on bough
Doth sweetly sing to me of her I love ;
The lark trills out my rapture with his own,
And heaven itself hath borrowed from my dear
Her azure eyes serene to give me light.
In all things fair I see her, hear her, love her !—
And lived she not, then lived they not for me ! ...
What power hath this gentlest mood of all !
My heart that never quailed in fight or tilt,
Though menaced times and scores of times with
      death—
If one but speak my lady's name !—this heart

Starts like a troutlet in yon stream, and all
The current of my life is stirred with joy !
But, damsel, since ye need no aid from me,
And since my gracious mistress waits for me,
I go to win her honour, as I hope.
O wish me well ! and may your own fair face
Both light and loadstar be to him ye love
For ever, as my lady's is to me !"

Thereat with low obeisance he passed
Out of her sight, and on to lands unknown ;
And with him passed the glory of the hour.
But barbèd memories of his speech remained
To prick Simplicita, perturb her mind,
And strike a hundred thousand petty flaws
Upon her morning's mood of smooth content.
Now all at once she saw herself, her fate ;
How blank a past—a future how unkind—
And the time present changeful as a dream !
And like a child upon its broken toy,
She gazed on what erewhile had made her bliss.

Yet none less blithely called the mounting
    finch,
The sky was all as blue, the flowers as sweet

As when she woke at dawn, and through the
    fields
Moved ever by her side the Silent Knight.
Then came the thought, " Can this be all in life ?
And shall I never know a fuller joy ?
Never be loved as other women are ?
And die unsought, unhonoured and alone ? "
She shivered, for the day had chilled, there
    rose
A little cloud about the sun, the Knight
Moved in the shade, his shining armour dulled,
His plumes blown grey and thin like vapour
    tossed
And all his look grown wan.   Then through a
    screen
Of willow-boughs across the stream, came sound
Of voices singing where upon the banks
A lusty shepherd and his lass had tryst :

    " When Dian leads her silver sheep
    To pasture them in fields divine,
    And winds do shear them where they shine,
    And whirl above the farmer's roof
    Their unsubstantial fleeces fine ;
    When weary lids are kissed by sleep,
    And dreams keep watch o'er closèd eyne,

Wilt thou for ever shine aloof?
O lady mine ! O lady mine !"

Thus sang the shepherd trolling out the words,
And treble tones then took the ditty up :

"The maiden moon once left her sheep
To whisper in a shepherd's ear,
And lest the little stars might hear,
She bade the laughing winds to blow ;
But lo ! the nested nightingale
Upon its wedding-bough was near,
And sang so loud the pretty tale,
That all the world hath learnt it now.
Since all the pretty tale do know
That Dian whispered on the steep,
To give her gentle shepherd cheer,
Wilt thou for ever silence keep?
My lover dear ! My lover dear !"

O what a niggard world is this of ours !
Here's not enough of bliss for all ; the thing
We make our stepping-stone to joy may prove
A stumbling-block to others' happiness !
"Wilt thou for ever shine aloof? Wilt thou
For ever silence keep ?"—these idle lines

O'er which the clownish lovers laughed and
      kissed,
Swelled the meek bosom of Simplicita,
Bore down her caution, beat about her heart,
Till all her gathered passion burst its dam.
" O thou !" she cried, " whom I have followed
      thus
Through fairy-land, hast thou no care for me?
No voice to tell me whence thou art ?—no joy
In aught but soulless things.   Lo ! now my life
Is weary.   Human hearts must feed on more
Than beauty, be it ne'er so beautiful ;
And mine would fain have something of its own.
Speak, therefore, Knight, and say thou lovest
      me !"
Then the earth yawned or so it seemed ; the
      wind
Laughed fiercely overhead and boughs convulsed
Beat wildly down between her and the Knight ;
And all was pain and chaos ; but she saw
In his clear eyes immeasurable scorn,
And saw him then no more.

             A band of men
Urging o'erridden horses galloped up
And hemmed her in upon the reeling ground ;

And one from saddle rolling, in a voice
That brought the loathèd past about her ears,
Roared " Halt ! " and barred the way.

                       Her kinsman 'twas,
Who with his knights had scoured the land since
        dawn
In vain pursuit, and now at last informed
By one that early came to tend the flocks,
Set spur and leaped on her where two roads met.
Here, face to face with nobles of her court,
Whose flushed and frowning foreheads and fierce
        eyes
Added fresh terrors to the strident tones
Of their amazèd questions ;—dumb she stood,
With vacant looks like one aroused from sleep ;
Till, seeing she answered not, disdainfully
They tossed her on her kinsman's steaming horse
And turned them back to palace through the
        trees.
Then blank despair o'ercame Simplicita
Half-swooning in her loveless wooer's arms ;
Thereafter too, with fever gripped, she hung
For many weary weeks 'twixt life and death,
And thence by slow degrees her gentle soul
Sank deep and deeper into childishness.

For she was gentle ever, though she grew
To loathe all sound, and times with queenly air
Provoking smiles, forbade her ladies speech ;
But oftener paced her garden ways and wept,
And cried out "hush !" to little piping birds,
And bade the winds and babbling stream be still
And "Silence, silence !" called, till those who
        watched
Feared her weak breath would rave itself away.

But all was still at last.   Upon a day
That winds were stripping off the useless leaves,
And drifts of wandering wings beflecked the sky :
And there came moving clouds and farewell
        cries,
And sweet and solemn hurry in the air,
As though the year were gathering up its skirts
Regretfully, on its long journey bent,
Against the chinks of her unopening door
The jester sate, his foolish face all tears,
And knew the end was nigh.

                    Beside him crouched
Simplicita's great hound, with restless ears
Marking each sound within, and now and then
As fitful steps drew near and mocked his wish

The hound sprang quivering up ; but as they
    passed
Dejected sank again in feigned repose.
And while they watched and feared, poor faith-
    ful hearts !
And night and anguish deeper grew, came one
Who longer yet had watched Simplicita ;
And he, 'gainst whom no doors prevail, went in
And laid a quiet hand upon her heart.   •

Then broke the morn—then were the gates flung
    wide—
Then came the people bringing woven boughs
To deck their Princess dead, and whispering
    hung
About the stair in awe ;—for Death who makes
Heroic marble of our human clay,
With cold and kindly finger had composed
Her childish face in such majestic peace,
That those who saw her lying there at rest—
Crowned with the gold of autumn woods and
    tall
Beyond their thought of her in life—were smit
With vague remorse, as though of treason done
To her great sire, and mourned her as their
    Queen.

And all that heavy dawn and all the day
The bells tolled slowly for Simplicita ;
But on the next as she was borne away
To burial upon an open bier,
In reverence of her cry for silence, past,
Their iron-throated sobbing ceased ; nor might
The roll of drum be heard, nor music drear,
Nor any sound, save only muffled tramp
Of crowds that dumbly thronged her funeral
        train,
'Neath thund'rous skies that yet forbore to break.
But round the darkling abbey arches beat
Tones ominous, and gathering sounds of storm
When those who lingered o'er the last sad rites
Veiled her sweet face and sealed her golden head
Fast in the silence of the tomb for ever.